Title: Dinosaurs Are Scary!
Author and Illustrator: Daesol Kim
Editor: Daesol Kim
Front Cover and Book Design: Daesol Kim

ISBN 9798362927035

Dinosaurs r scary!

Written and Illustrated by Daesol Kim

Dinosaurs are scary!

They are... mean and green!

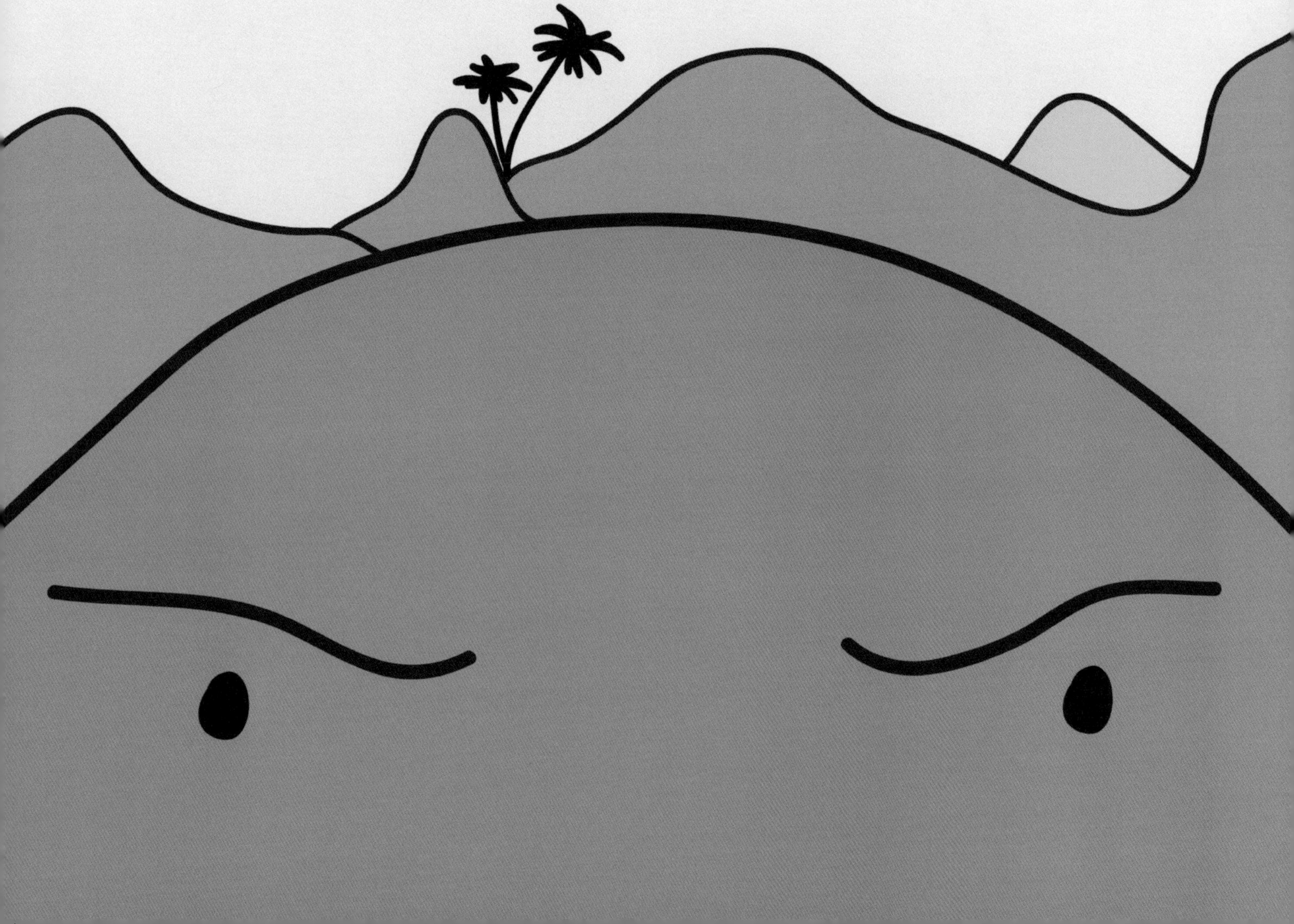

They have... tiny ferocious eyes!

They have... massive monstrous claws!

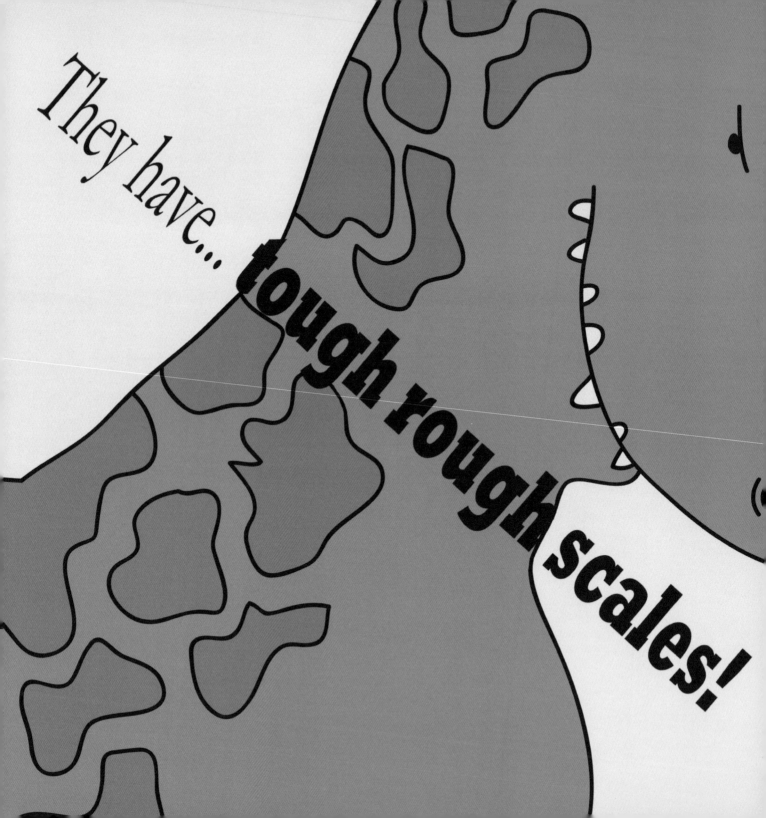

But what if we gave them...

a lovely dress?

They would look so pretty!

What if we gave them...

massive glasses?

They would have the cutest eyes!

What if we gave them...

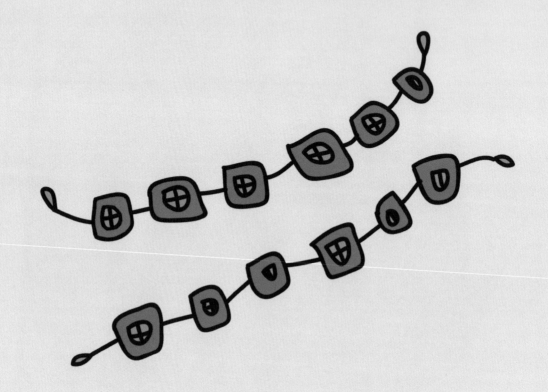

colourful braces?

They would have the friendliest set of teeth!

What if we gave them...

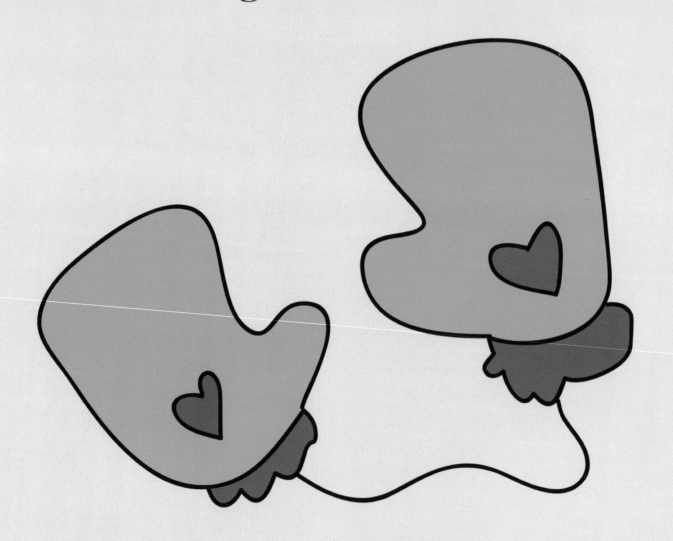

fluffy mittens?

They would have the softest hands!

What if we gave them...

clunky roller-skates?

They would be the best dancers!

What if we gave them...

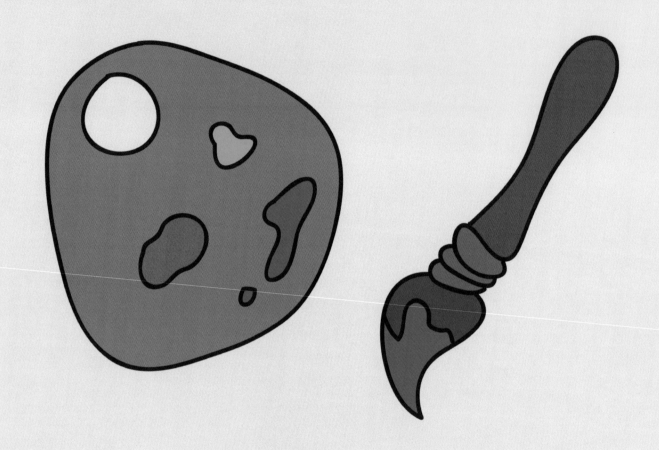

a paint-over?

They would have the coolest scales!

What if we gave them...

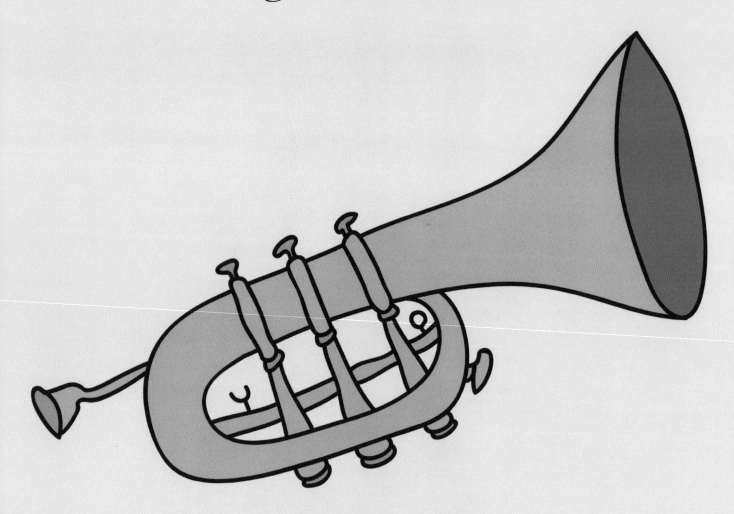

a golden trumpet?

They would play the most beautiful tune!

Dinosaurs aren't so scary anymore!

Printed in Great Britain
by Amazon

13295127R00018